THE MILLS & BOON®
MODERN GIRL'S GUIDE TO
Happy Endings

HQ
An imprint of HarperCollinsPublishers Ltd.
1 London Bridge Street
London SE1 9GF

This hardback edition 2017

1
First published in Great Britain by
HQ, an imprint of HarperCollinsPublishers Ltd. 2017

A catalogue record for this book is
available from the British Library

ISBN: 978-0-00-821236-0

Printed and bound in Italy

Funny, feisty and feminist:
The Mills & Boon Modern Girl's Survival Guides.

Introduction

Céline Dion confidently predicted that her heart would go on, even if, from a medical perspective, the romance between Kate and Leo was dead in the freezing North Atlantic waters. The sea of love can be a lot like that: full of unexpected icebergs in the shape of disapproving parents, interfering friends, unwarranted advances from co-workers and unexplainably odd matches on dating apps.

There's no denying that it's choppy out there, and if you're looking for love (or just someone to while away the long, dark, lonely evenings with until something better turns up), you're going to have deal with some bad stuff: unrequited crushes, rubbish boyfriends and the kind of outings that may leave permanent scars – actual scars, like a bad tattoo with both your names entwined in a gothic heart, or mental scars, like choosing 'Blurred Lines' as 'your song' before you'd actually worked out what the lyrics meant.

And once you've found love? Well, it's not all plain sailing in the love boat. There's infidelity, jealousy, arguments, and Ikea, and that's often before you actually get to know them.

But still, the heart wants what the heart wants, and this entirely positive and optimistic guide to relationships will steer you through the ups and downs of romance. Or at least guide you into the arms of a black-hearted pirate who knows where the treasure is buried.

nniversaries

Anniversary Gift Guide (Probably):

1 year – Paper

2 years – Cotton

5 years – Egg

6 years – Hopes pinned on gold,
turns out to be egg again

10 years – VHS tapes

15 years – Gummy sweet eternity ring

25 years – Channing Tatum trapped in amber

50 years – A withering glance

75 years – Two entire puppies

100 years – Back to paper

Biological Clock

Simone and Rosetta are worried
about their biological clocks.

But they're more worried about how close they are
to killing the next person who reminds them that
time is not on their side.

They have made a yodelling meter. Partly to distract
them from the remorseless tick-tocking, but mostly
to drown out the perpetual questions about their
currently empty wombs.

Bunny Girl

'I'm really sorry I scared you. It was supposed to be a sexy surprise! Like a bunny girl thing?

No, I know rabbits don't hatch out of eggs. It made sense in my head.'

Colleague

Ideas for How to Hide from Harry
After Friday's Office Drinks:

Never go to work again, live off savings
(no savings, obviously)

Get radical haircut
(not just my head he'll recognise)

Furiously avoid eye contact
(has eyes the colour of the deepest ocean,
literally can't not look at them. That was the
trouble in the first place)

Head-to-toe fancy dress
(bingo!)

Dating Apps

What They Say:

'Our unique algorithm will use a range of
metrics to find your perfect match'

What They Mean:

'Our unpaid intern will pull names out of a bin,
and you'll end up with some hat collecting freak.'

Dropping Hints

Ways in Which Shelia Has Tried to Let Kevin
Know She's Keen, Which Have Somehow Failed
to Do the Job:

'Jokingly' referring to their being like
'an old married couple' then fixing him with a
serious stare and whispering: 'I would so marry you'

'Liking' every single tweet he has ever sent,
even the boring political ones

Semaphore

Touching her hair a lot

Exes

Some might call her paranoid, but Daphne couldn't shake the feeling that she was failing to measure up to Max's first wife.

Fictional Boyfriend

Amy's boyfriend is definitely real, you just haven't seen him around because he goes to a different school, in Canada, because he's Canadian.

He lives in the middle of a forest and makes wooden bowls and is very sensitive, and also he has great muscle definition and *loves kissing Amy*.

He is absolutely not a tiny stuffed puppet in a pointy hat.

Amy can one hundred per cent guarantee that.

Future Plans

Mary and Joseph have a vision of kids,
a dog, and a nice home in the countryside.

Being millennials, there's no way they will ever be able to remotely afford any of these things, so they are going to live in a tiny rented studio flat and 'look after' these unsettling plastic models for the next forty years.

irlfriends

Francine: Woooo! We are the ghosts of Liam's girlfriends past, come to warn you against getting mixed up with him.

Sarah: Francine, you aren't dead. Neither are you, Suzanne. I literally just saw you in John Lewis buying the curtain you're hiding behind.

Francine: This isn't a curtain; it's the veil that separates the living from the dead, woooo hooo. Liam is baaaad news.

Sarah: Look, girls, I know you don't like Liam, but this is ridiculous.

Happily Ever After

Top 5 Unrealistic Expectations Set by
Fairy Tales Which Continue to Disappoint:

5) Prince Charming

4) Fairy Godmother

3) Free pumpkin taxis

2) Years and years of uninterrupted sleep

1) Woodland animals cleaning your flat

ipster

Cons:

Stupid clothes

Makes you go to pop-ups

Insists on using a typewriter because it
'puts him in touch with the spirit of Hemingway'
and he 'likes how tactile it is'

Pros:

At some point he will get his hand and/or wang
stuck in the mechanism

Worth sticking around for that alone

Ikea

On the one hand, Bernice is secretly pleased, because she knows that screaming blue murder at each other in the middle of Ikea is an important relationship milestone.

But on the other hand, Bernice really does think the *Krudsturm* is way too big for the kitchen.

Infidelity

Signs he might be cheating on you with that sheep:

Stays late at work

Faint smell of hay

Makes you call him 'Bo'

Has started watching *Countryfile*

In-Laws

Clara's Top Three Disturbing
Things About Hugh's Family:

3. The way his mum keeps glancing Clara's way and saying to no one in particular: 'Well, I suppose the important thing is that HUGH likes her'

2. The incomprehensible board game they insist on playing every Christmas

1. The fridge that's entirely full of butter and nothing else

Jealousy

Leave it, Darren.

Kink

'Seriously, Phil, what is up with you trying to get me to eat apples all the time? Every day, the same thing: *"Why not eat a load of apples? Try some delicious apples?"* It's *weird*.

'I figure either you work for the apple marketing board or you're a *feeder*, one of those guys who gets off by transforming his girlfriend into a fuller figured woman.

'And I am *definitely* on-board with that, but I think we'll get there a lot faster with massive bits of cake.'

Losing the Spark

Signs the Spark Might Have Gone from Your Relationship:

Partner hasn't laughed at your jokes lately

Partner has stopped complimenting your appearance

Partner has tied you to a conveyor belt heading towards three enormous spinning blades

Partner seems emotionally distant

Love Triangle

Henry loves Julie.

Julie loves Eileen.

Eileen is in a committed relationship
with this ice cream.

Making a Move

Millie has been trying to kiss Mike for weeks.

If this spaghetti trick doesn't work, like it worked for that stupid animated dog, then she's packing up and moving to Newfoundland where she will stare mournfully at icebergs for the rest of her life.

Mansplaining

Sarah Guppy is on a date with Mr Mann, who has been very slowly explaining things to her for the past hour.

MM: 'This . . . is . . . a . . . picture . . . of . . . the . . . Clifton . . . Suspension . . . Bridge. Cars . . . go . . . over . . . it.'

SG: 'Yes, I know, I filed the patent for the chain technology it uses in 1811.'

MM: 'The . . . river . . . goes . . . under . . . the . . . bridge.'

Marital Bliss

Geraldine has combined her twin interests of 'smashing the patriarchy' and 'advanced taxidermy' by getting herself a trophy husband.

Negging

Simon had obviously read one of those books about negging, but Angela didn't have the heart to tell him that he was getting it quite badly wrong.

And besides, Angela liked eggs, so what the hell.

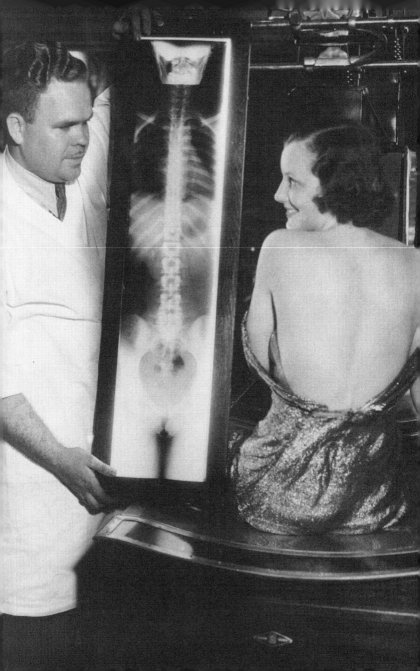

Opportunist

'So, to conclude, your lower vertebrae
have healed nicely.

'Now, how's about that lovely back of yours
joins me for dinner tonight . . . ?'

Other Couples

Gavin and Marge have failed to recognise exactly how much their constant public displays of affection are getting on everyone's nerves.

Peer Pressure

Stevie is on her way to the annual village fête. According to her friends, loads of cool guys from the next village are going to be there.

Stevie was perfectly happy alone at home and suspects that a cool guy would just clog up her sofa, so she's dressed as a lettuce and plans to hide in the vegetable tent.

Pick Up Artists

'Take it from me, mate, you've got to attract a girl's attention as soon as you walk in. Then - BAM! - she'll be eating out of the palm of your hand.'

'Couldn't I just wear an interesting jacket or something?'

'It's called "peacocking" for a reason, Steve.'

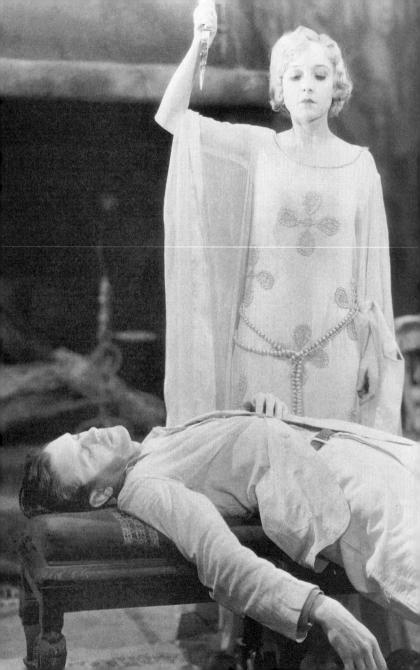

uickie

George thinks he and Claire just had
a really sexy quickie, like in porn.

George is wrong on pretty much every level.

Reasonable discussion

'Let's discuss it when we get home.'

'No, I want to talk about it NOW.'

'Well I don't.'

'Well I DO.'

'Stop SHOUTING at me.'

'I AM NOT SHOUTING.'

Shared Interests

Helen dearly wishes she could list 'Food' or 'Books' as hobbies and interests on her Tinder profile.

But unfortunately, they fall on the 'Men' side of the big rubber ring, so she has had to stick to 'Lingerie' and 'Miscellaneous'.

Spin the Bottle

Please no

Surprise

Trish held her breath.

Colin may have brought her many happy years,
but if this turned out to be another bloody towel
rack he'd be out on his ear.

Texting

Dawn stares at the third draft of her text to Gary, wondering if *'Yo Gaz-matazz'* would be a better, more casual sounding opening than *'Hello there, my good man'*, and, with a heavy sigh, presses delete.

'Fourth time's the charm!' she thinks.

Third Wheel

Martin insists on bringing Chad, his two-hundred-pound carp, to every date.

Justine is starting to wonder if maybe *she* is the gooseberry.

Totally Over Him

Emma doesn't think about Roberto at all these days.

He literally never crosses her mind.

Especially since she's thrown herself into all these fun extra-curricular activities.

Like the art classes. They really keep her occupied.

She only paints his face over and over again whilst sobbing into the canvas because he has such an interesting bone structure.

Unwanted Advances

Diane had her headphones on *specifically* so she could avoid getting chatted up by strange men, but Don has read an article about how to do a clever mime in order to get her to take them off.

Don has done this so he can tell Diane that a girl as pretty as her should *smile* more.

Diane is very impressed by this strategy and is probably going to sleep with Don right there, in the middle of the street.

Look, you can see it on her face.

alentine

<u>Evidence for this being a</u>
<u>Valentine's card from Roland:</u>

He looked at her in the lift yesterday.

He almost sat next to her at the after-work drinks.

Is she imagining things, or does
it *smell* just like him?

<u>Evidence against this being a Valentine's</u>
<u>card from Roland:</u>

It's the electricity bill.

 Wrong end of the stick

Colin, I'm going to say this one more time:
you are not my type.

X-rated

It's great that Ray wants to spice
things up in bed.

And his idea for 'a bit of role-play'
did sound fun.

But whatever the hell this is
supposed to be, it isn't doing it for me.

Your Friends Setting You Up

'Duncan's great! You'll love him.'

'I'm not sure he's exactly my type. I just find the beak a turn-off. And the . . . that bit on his neck?'

'His wattle?'

'Yeah, I'm not really into the wattle either.'

'Stop being so *shallow*. You're so obsessed by *looks*. Duncan's really interesting. Plus, you're not getting any younger, you know. Look, here he is now.'

'Oh God.'

Zsa Zsa's Life Advice

'A girl must marry for love,
and keep on marrying until she finds it.'

-Zsa Zsa Gabor, film star. Married nine times

About Ada Adverse

Ada has been married eight times, including, on one occasion
in the early 90's, to a rock – a full twenty years, you'll note,
before Tracy Emin came up with the same idea. Unlucky in love,
all of Ada's partners have died in tragic circumstances,
mostly unexplained fires.

Ada's interests include life insurance policies,
petrol and topical poisons.

About Mills & Boon®

Since 1908, Mills & Boon® have been a girl's best friend.

We've seen a lot change in the years since: enjoying sex as a woman is now not only officially fine but actively encouraged, dry shampoo has revolutionised our lives and, best of all, we've come full circle on gin.

But being a woman still has its challenges. We're under-paid, exhaustingly objectified, and under-represented at top tables. We work for free from 19th November, and our life-choices are scrutinised and forever found lacking. Plus: PMS; unsolicited d*ck pics; the price of tights.

Sometimes, a girl just needs a break.
And, for a century, that's where we've come in.

So, to celebrate one hundred years of wisdom (or at least a lot of fun), we've produced these handy A-Zs: funny, feisty, feminist guides to help the modern girl get through the day.

We can't promise an end to the bullsh*t.
But we can offer some light relief along the way.